W9-AOE-855

10/2015

DISCARD

Dear Parent:

Congratulations! Your child is taking the first steps on an exciting journey. The destination? Independent reading!

STEP INTO READING® will help your child get there. The program offers five steps to reading success. Each step includes fun stories and colorful art. There are also Step into Reading Sticker Books, Step into Reading Math Readers, Step into Reading Phonics Readers, Step into Reading Write-In Readers, and Step into Reading Phonics Boxed Sets—a complete literacy program with something to interest every child.

Learning to Read, Step by Step!

Ready to Read   Preschool–Kindergarten
• big type and easy words • rhyme and rhythm • picture clues
For children who know the alphabet and are eager to begin reading.

Reading with Help   Preschool–Grade 1
• basic vocabulary • short sentences • simple stories
For children who recognize familiar words and sound out new words with help.

Reading on Your Own   Grades 1–3
• engaging characters • easy-to-follow plots • popular topics
For children who are ready to read on their own.

Reading Paragraphs   Grades 2–3
• challenging vocabulary • short paragraphs • exciting stories
For newly independent readers who read simple sentences with confidence.

Ready for Chapters   Grades 2–4
• chapters • longer paragraphs • full-color art
For children who want to take the plunge into chapter books but still like colorful pictures.

STEP INTO READING® is designed to give every child a successful reading experience. The grade levels are only guides. Children can progress through the steps at their own speed, developing confidence in their reading, no matter what their grade.

Remember, a lifetime love of reading starts with a single step!

Special thanks to Sarah Buzby, Cindy Ledermann, Vicki Jaeger, Dana Koplik, Ann McNeill, Emily Kelly, Sharon Woloszyk, Julia Phelps, Tanya Mann, Rob Hudnut, David Wiebe, Tiffany J. Shuttleworth, Gabrielle Miles, Rainmaker Entertainment, Walter P. Martishius, Carla Alford, Rita Lichtwardt, and Kathy Berry

Visit us on the Web!
StepIntoReading.com
randomhouse.com/kids
www.barbie.com

Educators and librarians, for a variety of teaching tools, visit us at randomhouse.com/teachers

ISBN 978-0-307-93004-0 (trade) — ISBN 978-0-375-97004-7 (lib. bdg.)
Printed in the United States of America   10 9 8 7 6 5 4 3

Random House Children's Books supports the First Amendment and celebrates the right to read.

STEP INTO READING®

STEP 2

Barbie in A Mermaid Tale 2

Surf Princess

Adapted by Chelsea Eberly

Based on the original screenplay by Elise Allen

Illustrated by Ulkutay Design Group

Random House 🏠 New York

Merliah
and Kylie
love surfing.
They both want
to be the best.

Merliah has
a secret.

She is half mermaid!

Her mother
is Calissa.
She is the queen
of Oceana.
Merliah visits Calissa.

Calissa shows Merliah
a royal ceremony.

It keeps the ocean alive.

The next ceremony
is the same day as
the big surfing contest.
Merliah cannot go.
Calissa is sad.
Merliah swims home.

Merliah and Kylie
both surf
in the big contest.

Merliah gets
all the attention.
Kylie is jealous.

Kylie meets
a rainbow fish
named Alistair.
He says that
Merliah's necklace
has special powers.

Kylie takes

the necklace.

Kylie puts
on the necklace.
She turns
into a mermaid!

She follows Alistair
into the ocean.

Alistair traps Kylie
in a whirlpool.
Merliah's evil aunt
Eris is set free.

Merliah cannot find
her necklace.

Snouts the sea lion
takes Merliah to Kylie.

Merliah ties herself
to a rock.
She dives
into the whirlpool.
She saves Kylie!

Calissa gets ready
for the royal ceremony.

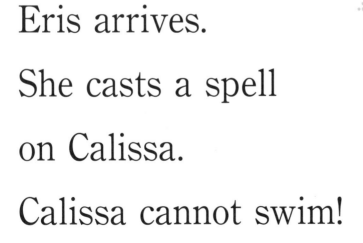

Eris arrives.

She casts a spell
on Calissa.

Calissa cannot swim!

Merliah has a plan.

Kylie will help.

So will Snouts

and Zuma the dolphin!

Merliah and Kylie
rope two big fish.
They ride them
like horses!

Kylie bumps Eris
off the throne.
Merliah is the real
princess!

Merliah sits
on the throne.
Kylie gives her
necklace back.

Merliah sparkles.
She turns into
a beautiful mermaid.

The ceremony worked!

The ocean is saved.

The spell on Calissa
is broken.
It is cast on Eris.
Her tail turns to legs.

Calissa thanks
Merliah and Kylie
for saving the ocean.
Then the girls leave
for the surfing contest.

Merliah has fun surfing!
She does not care
about winning.
Protecting the ocean
is her dream now!

Kylie wins!
Merliah is happy
for her new friend.